MY 20 '97   NoAR

√P

BILLINGS CO SCHOOLS LIBRARY

P9-AES-628

80.

E Lebrun
Lebrun, Claude.
Little Brown Bear plays in
the snow

WITHDRAWN
DICKINSON AREA PUBLIC LIBRARY

No AR test

LITTLE BROWN BEAR
Plays in the Snow

Written by Claude Lebrun

Illustrated by Danièle Bour

Billings County Public School Dist. No. 1
Box 307
Medora, North Dakota 58645

 Children's Press®

A Division of Grolier Publishing
New York   London   Hong Kong   Sydney
Danbury, Connecticut

Little Brown Bear
plays in the snow.
He makes
a little snowball.

He rolls it
and he rolls it
until it is
bigger than he is!

Next,
Little Brown Bear
makes three
little snowballs.
He throws one.

It lands right on
Papa Bear's nose.
"I'm sorry, Papa,"
Little Brown Bear says.

Billings County Public School Dist. No. 7
Box 307
Medora, North Dakota   58645

Little Brown Bear
lies down
in the soft snow.

When he gets up,
he sees what
he has made—
a little white bear
in the snow.

Little Brown Bear
licks the snow.
It is wet and cold,
like an
ice-cream cone.

This series was produced by Mijo Beccaria.

The illustrations were created by Danièle Bour.

The text was written by Claude Lebrun and
edited by Pomme d'Api.

English translation by Children's Press.

Library of Congress Cataloging–in–Publication Data
Lebrun, Claude.
Little Brown Bear plays in the snow / written by Claude Lebrun:
illustrated by Danièle Bour.
p. cm. — (Little Brown Bear books)
Summary: Little Brown Bear makes snowballs
and does other fun things in the snow.
ISBN 0-516-07847-X (School & Library Edition)
ISBN 0-516-17847-4 (Trade Edition)
ISBN 0-516-17805-9 (Boxed Set)
[1. Bears — Fiction. 2. Snow — Fiction.] I. Bour, Danièle, ill.
II. Title. III. Series: Lebrun, Claude. Little Brown Bear books.

PZ7.L4698Lnf   1996
[E] — dc20   95-26330
                                                                  CIP
                                                                   AC

English translation ©1997 by Children's Press
A Division of Grolier Publishing Co., Inc., Sherman Turnpike, Danbury, Connecticut 06813
Originally published in French by Bayard.
All rights reserved.
Published simultaneously in Canada.
Printed in Belgium
1 2 3 4 5 6 7 8 9 00 R 06 05 04 03 02 01 00 99 98 97